WARNING FROM THE WAVES

BY JUSTINE SMITH
ILLUSTRATED BY CHARLOTTE ALDER

Librarian Reviewer
Marci Peschke
Librarian, Dallas Independent School District
MA Education Reading Specialist, Stephen F. Austin State University
Learning Resources Endorsement, Texas Women's University

Reading Consultant
Sherry Klehr
Elementary/Middle School Educator, Edina Public Schools, MN
MA in Education, University of Minnesota

 **STONE ARCH BOOKS**
Minneapolis   San Diego

First published in the United States in 2008
by Stone Arch Books
151 Good Counsel Drive, P.O. Box 669
Mankato, Minnesota 56002
www.stonearchbooks.com

Originally published in Great Britain in 2006
by Badger Publishing Ltd

Library of Congress Cataloging-in-Publication Data
Smith, Justine.
    [Mer-boy]
    Warning from the Waves / by Justine Smith; illustrated by Charlotte
Alder.
    p. cm. — (Keystone books)
    ISBN 978-1-4342-0475-2 (library binding)
    ISBN 978-1-4342-0525-4 (paperback)
    [1. Mermen—Fiction.] I. Alder, Charlotte, ill. II. Title.
PZ7.S65217War 2008
[Fic]—dc22   2007028517

1 2 3 4 5 6 13 12 11 10 09 08

Printed in the United States of America

TABLE OF CONTENTS

- Chapter 1 -

THE BOAT

Tara grew up by the sea. She had always loved the water.

"You are my little mermaid," her mother would say.

"More like a smelly fish!" teased Alisha, Tara's best friend.

Alisha and Tara were very different. Alisha was loud and crazy, and Tara was the quiet one. But it worked. They did everything together.

They listened to music, watched television, and rode around on their bikes. They had a lot of fun.

They were like sisters.

The two girls stood and looked down at the boats. "Come on, let's do it!" said Alisha.

Tara shook her hair out of her eyes and gave her friend a look.

"What?" said Alisha. "What's the problem?"

Alisha always looked like the nicest, sweetest girl in the world.

She had soft, black curly hair that she always wore in braids.

Her dark, sparkling eyes showed her fun, playful, crazy side.

Alisha's middle name was Trouble.

Tara thought for a moment. They were both good swimmers. She was sure it would be safe.

"Okay," she said.

As the friends got into the boat, the wind began to blow. Tara felt cold.

Chapter 2

A SUDDEN SPLASH

It was fun in the boat. Soon, Tara stopped worrying.

"Me first!" said Alisha. She took the oars. It was easy. The boat slid along the water, fast and smooth.

"This is so cool!" Alisha said.

Tara put her fingers in the water. She smiled. She felt sleepy. She looked over the side and down into the darkness.

Suddenly, Tara sat up. "What's that in the water?" she shouted.

Alisha jumped. She dropped an oar just as a gust of wind blew across the water. The boat rocked.

"Watch out!" shouted Alisha.

But it was too late. Tara was falling into the water!

Chapter 3

THE SONG

Tara hit the water. As her head went under, everything went still.

Then she heard a sound far away.

Was it Alisha?

The boat floated above her.

It would be easy to swim up to it. She kicked her legs.

But, just then, Tara felt something grab her hand.

"Stay," sang a watery voice. It sounded like silver bells.

"Listen," sang the voice.

Tara frowned.

What was the voice saying? It seemed important.

The song was all around Tara. She was happy to stay in the water, like a fish, and listen.

And then a weird thing happened: Tara saw a face that she knew.

Chapter 4

AN OLD FRIEND

A pair of bright, sea-green eyes blinked open in front of her.

It was a boy. He was about her age.

Tara's eyes opened wide.

She smiled.

"It's you," she said.

Everything seemed to stop.

All her life, Tara had felt close to the ocean. She had loved splashing in the waves when she was a little girl.

One day she had seen the boy under the water. She thought it was a dream.

Ever since then, she had looked for him by the ocean and dreamed of him at night.

In her dreams he took her to his home, and showed her his sea-garden, and they played with the dolphins and baby seals.

He was her special secret, but she had never seen him again.

Until now.

The boy was trying to tell her something.

"Come with me," he sang. He took her hand.

"Just for a while," she said.

The boy pulled at her hand again.

But then Tara remembered Alisha.

"I have to go," she said. She swam back up to the boat.

"I have to tell you something," sang the boy. "Something important."

But Tara couldn't turn around.

Chapter 5

MYSTERY MESSAGE

The sun came out, and Tara dried off in the boat.

"How long was I under the water?" asked Tara. It had felt like hours.

Alisha gave her a funny look. "About a second!" she said. "But you scared me. Try not to fall in again!"

"Listen. I have to tell you something," said Tara. She told her friend about the boy.

Alisha listened. She didn't say a word.

"I know it sounds really weird," said Tara. "But it did happen. It really did! He was trying to tell me something. Please believe me!"

She looked at her friend.

Alisha smiled. "Of course I believe you, silly," she said. "But what I want to know is, what was he trying to tell you?"

The friends talked it over for hours. They couldn't figure out what the boy had wanted.

Later, the two girls walked home from the beach, arm in arm, tired and happy.

Chapter 6

DREAM

That night, Tara had the dream about the boy again.

In her dream, a boat rocked on a wild and stormy sea.

Tara heard the boy's voice singing.

It wasn't the first time Tara had that dream, but this time she could hear what his song said.

She could hear it loud and clear.

* * *

The next day, the two friends were sitting in a restaurant.

"Tell me again," said Alisha.

"Well," Tara said slowly. "In the dream I'm under the water and there are rocks all around me. There's this voice. It says, 'Turn on the light.'"

"What do you think it means?" asked Alisha.

"I don't know," said Tara. "But it has to mean something. I have the same dream every night."

"We'll just have to go down to the beach again tomorrow," said Alisha. "We'll find the boy. I'll ask him myself!"

Tara laughed.

She felt better.

But Alisha never got to ask her question.

That night, as Tara slept, a huge storm came.

The storm grew.

The wind blew angrily over the sea and around the houses.

It howled all night, and rain poured down.

Tara woke up.

Suddenly, she knew what the dream meant. She knew what she had to do.

Chapter 7

THE STORM

First Tara ran to the window. She needed to check.

Then she ran to wake up her parents.

At first her mom thought Tara was having a bad dream. Then her dad thought it was a joke. "A very bad joke, at two in the morning," he said.

"Go back to bed, honey," said her mother, more kindly.

"Please, Dad! Just look out the window!" she said.

At last, Tara's dad got up. He stared out at the night. He scratched his head.

"That's strange," he said.

Instead of the friendly beam of the lighthouse, he saw only black sky.

"The light is out at the lighthouse," Tara said. "Boats will sail onto the rocks. We have to turn on the light!"

"I'll call the coast guard," her dad said slowly.

But the storm had made the phone lines go down. No one could get a cell phone signal. Dad started to look worried.

Tara thought about her friend, the strange boy. She made up her mind. "I can't give up," she said to herself.

"Please, Dad!" Tara begged.

He nodded. "Okay, Tara," he said.

Chapter 8

MiDNiGHT MiSSiON

It seemed to Tara that her dad's car was pushing through a wall of water. Slowly, they drove through the pouring rain.

Every now and then, Tara could see the top of the lighthouse, lit up by a flash of lightning.

They drove on, through the heart of the storm.

Would they ever make it?

Suddenly the lighthouse was right in front of them. Everything seemed to speed up. Tara's dad banged on the door.

No one answered. Then he kicked it down.

Inside, the lighthouse man was lying on the floor.

Then there were phone calls, shouting, and the flashing lights of the ambulance.

The lighthouse man had gotten sick and had not turned on the light.

There were so many people talking, Tara's dad, the doctors, the police, and the coast guard officers.

Finally, to Tara's relief, she saw the friendly beam of the lighthouse sweep across the ocean.

The beam lit up the rocks. A little boat was spinning in the stormy sea, but it was safe now.

Once it was all over, it almost seemed like a dream to Tara.

Chapter 9

FRiENDS FOREVER

One night, a few years later, Tara was leaving home for college. She went down to look at the ocean. A light danced on the water. Then she saw him, standing in the waves.

The silvery song was all around her. The boy laughed.

Tara looked into his sparkly eyes. She laughed too. She knew that he would always be part of her life.

"Goodbye for now," she said.

He waved, and turned, diving into the surf. She saw a flash of green tail.

And then he was gone.

About the Illustrator

Charlotte Alder has always worked in creative environments, but illustrating children's books is her favorite job. She says that her inspiration and best critics of her children's books are her nieces and nephews, who range in age from 3 to 14. She always gets honest answers from them! Charlotte lives in Devon, England, and she says, "For fresh ideas all I need to do is look out of my window or take a walk along the beach. It always seems to work!"

Glossary

beam (BEEM)—a ray or band of light

coast guard (KOHST gard)—the branch of a nation's armed forces that protects the coastline

gust (GUHST)—a sudden, strong blast of wind

howled (HOWLD)—cried out

lighthouse (LITE-houss)—a tower set in or near the sea. A lighthouse has a flashing light at the top that guides ships and warns them of danger.

mermaid (MUR-mayd)—an imaginary sea creature with the upper body of a woman and the tail of a fish

oar (OR)—a wooden pole with a flat blade at one end, used for rowing a boat

signal (SIG-nuhl)—a message or warning

sudden (SUHD-den)—without warning

wild (WILDE)—not controlled; crazy

Discussion Questions

1. How did Tara figure out what the boy's message meant?

2. The title of this book is *Warning From the Waves*. Can you think of any other titles that could work for this book? What does the title of this book mean?

3. In this book, Tara has to convince her parents that even though her dream sounded crazy, there is real danger. Have you ever had to convince a family member of something? What did you do? Did your convincing work?

Writing Prompts

1. Have you ever had a dream that seemed like it had a special message or predicted the future? What happened in your dream? Did it come true? Write about it.

2. In this book, Alisha and Tara are opposites. Is your best friend the same as you or different from you? Write about your differences and similarities.

3. At the end of the book, Tara says goodbye to the boy. Write a chapter that takes place when Tara comes home for a visit. What happens? Does she see the boy? Write it down!

If you liked this book . . .

Self Defender
by Jane West

Tess's new school seems okay, until a spiteful bully makes her school life miserable. Tess has to learn a new way to defend herself. Then she must wait until the moment that she can use her new skills!

The Messenger Bag
by Jillian Powell

Stacey is sick of her unstylish handbag. One day, Stacey finds a beautiful old Kelly bag. She takes it everywhere. The bag hides a secret that's meant only for Stacey.

. . . you'll love these, too!

MP3 Mind Control
by Jonny Zucker

Keisha's new MP3 player is really cool, but it seems to have a mind of its own. First it flashes strange numbers, and then it starts to steal Keisha's thoughts! What's at the bottom of this high-tech mystery?

The Star Key
by Melanie Joyce

On Tyler's thirteenth birthday she is given a strange note, written by her long-dead grandmother. Tyler learns that she has a special, secret destiny. Only she can save the world from terrible danger!

Internet Sites

Do you want to know more about subjects related to this book? Or are you interested in learning about other topics? Then check out FactHound, a fun, easy way to find Internet sites.

Our investigative staff has already sniffed out great sites for you!

Here's how to use FactHound:

1. Visit *www.facthound.com*

2. Select your grade level.

3. To learn more about subjects related to this book, type in the book's ISBN number: **9781434204752**

4. Click the **Fetch It** button.

FactHound will fetch the best Internet sites for you!